To
Jesse, Ricky, Big Nose, Rusty Boy, Raisin,
Bobby Dog, Zeker Boy, Betsy Higgins, Bugsey Bingus,
George Dog, and all dogs past and present
who judge a book by eating its cover.

—S.B. & S.B.

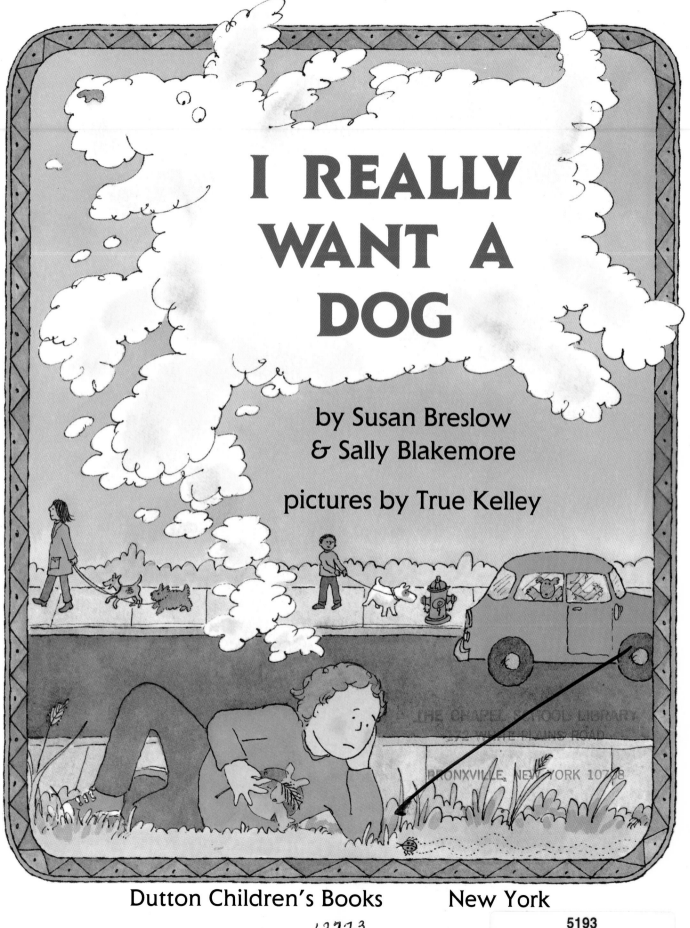

I REALLY WANT A DOG

by Susan Breslow
& Sally Blakemore

pictures by True Kelley

Dutton Children's Books   New York

I'd never
be sad.

I'd always
have someone
who loves me,
just me.

Me!

Sit

Lie down

Fetch

Good dog

Stay

Go
get a
dog!

Humongous

Shaggy

Curly

Sporty

Soulful

Friendly

Shy

Spotted

Two-toned

Frisky

Nervous

Fearless

Speedy

Long

Famous

Text copyright © 1990 by Susan Breslow and Sally Blakemore
Illustrations copyright © 1990 by True Kelley

All rights reserved.

Published in the United States by Dutton Children's Books,
a division of Penguin Books USA Inc.

Published simultaneously in Canada by
Fitzhenry & Whiteside Limited, Toronto

Designer: Martha Rago

Printed in Hong Kong by South China Printing Co.
First Edition   10 9 8 7 6 5 4 3 2 1

Library of Congress Cataloging-in-Publication Data
Breslow, Susan.
   I really want a dog/by Susan Breslow & Sally Blakemore;
pictures by True Kelley.—1st ed.
      p.   cm.
   Summary: A child explains how good he would be to a pet dog.
   ISBN 0-525-44589-7
   [1. Dogs—Fiction.]   I. Blakemore, Sally.   II. Kelley, True, ill.
III. Title.   89-38567
PZ7.B7546Iac   1990   CIP
[E]—dc20   AC